I WANNA IGUANA

BY T.E. WATSON
ILLUSTRATED BY JOHN RAPTIS

PAW PRINTS PRESS

This is for the super people who believed in me.
This book is dedicated to all of them.

T.E. Watson

To my Mom and Dad, who made sure I was never short
on drawing paper.

John Raptis

Text copyright © 2001 by T.E. Watson (Tom Watson)
Illustrations copyright © 2001 John Raptis
All rights reserved. Published by Paw Prints LLC.
An imprint of Highlander Celtic Publications.

ISBN 1-58478-009-6

Library of Congress Cataloging -in- Publication Data
Library of Congress Control Number 2001088565

Watson ,T.E.- Author
    I Wanna Iguana: A fictional picture book. Illustrations by John Raptis
Summary: A young boy's convincing reasons why he wants an iguana for a pet.
Pages: 32, Hardcover, Smythe Sewn, Color

Printed in Mexico. First Printing 2001

LET ME TELL YOU WHY I WANNA IGUANA.

WHEN YOU OWN AN IGUANA, IT'S LIKE HAVING YOUR OWN PERSONAL DINOSAUR.

IF I HAD AN IGUANA I WOULD TAKE VERY GOOD CARE OF IT.

I WANNA IGUANA BECAUSE
IGUANAS ARE REALLY FAST!

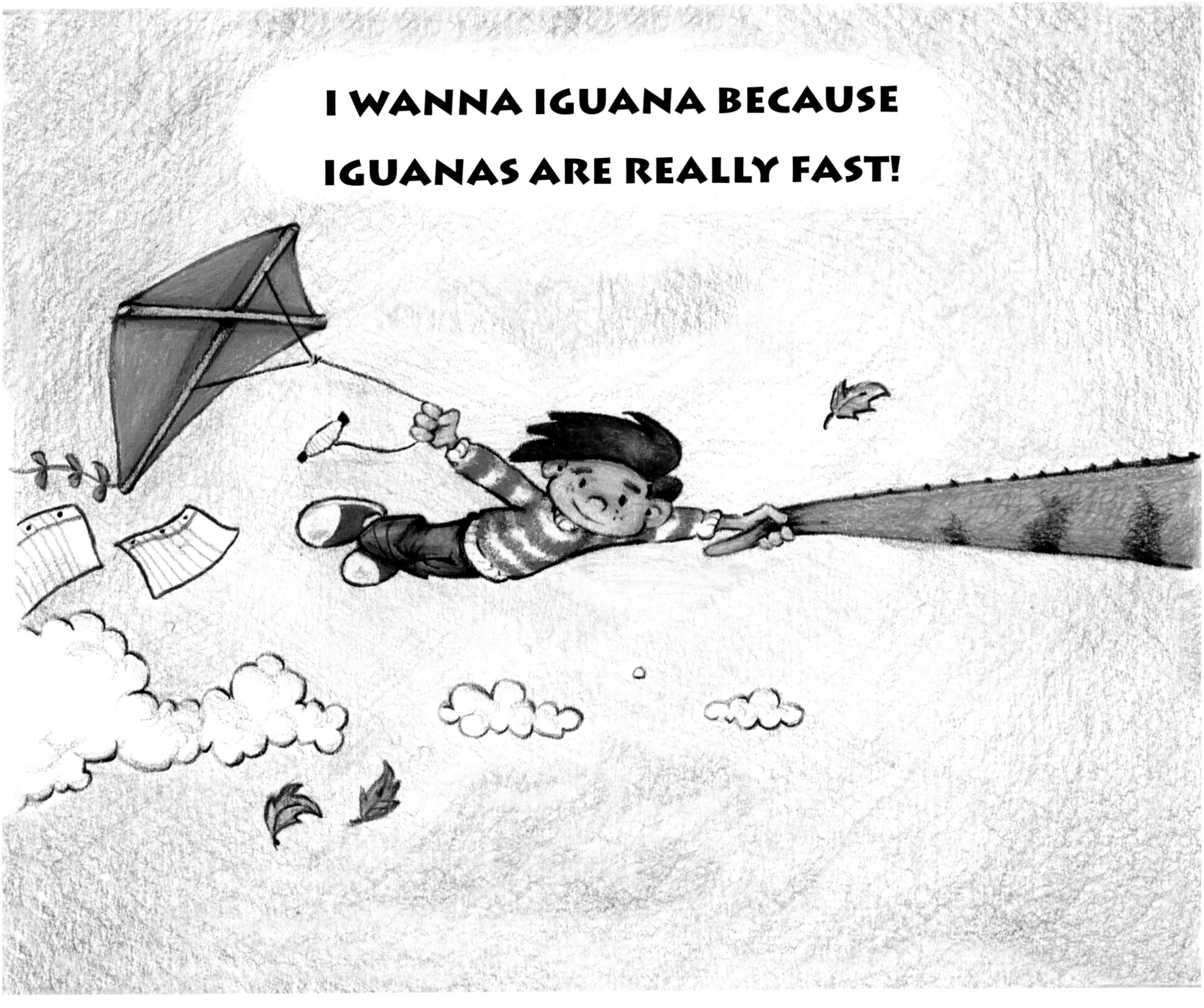

IF I HAD
AN IGUANA
FOR A PET
MY FRIENDS
WOULD COME
OVER AND
WE COULD
PLAY TOGETHER.

IGUANAS ARE NOT REAL MESSY AND THEY DON'T TAKE UP MUCH SPACE.

MY IGUANA COULD COME UP
TO MY TREE HOUSE FOR A VISIT.

I WOULD FEED MY IGUANA EVERYDAY.
THEY LIKE TO EAT FRUITS AND VEGETABLES
FROM THE MARKET. IT SHOULDN'T COST
TOO MUCH FOR GRAPES AND SPINACH.

WE COULD READ COMICS TOGETHER

MY FRIEND TONY HAS AN IGUANA.
HE GETS TO TAKE IT FOR RIDES
IN HIS DAD'S TRUCK.

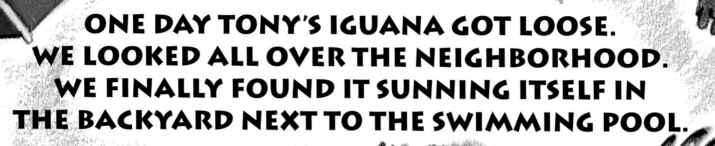

ONE DAY TONY'S IGUANA GOT LOOSE.
WE LOOKED ALL OVER THE NEIGHBORHOOD.
WE FINALLY FOUND IT SUNNING ITSELF IN
THE BACKYARD NEXT TO THE SWIMMING POOL.

IGUANAS LIVE IN
TREES IN THE
COUNTRY WHERE
THEY COME FROM.
THOSE TREES MUST
BE REALLY BIG!

MY IGUANA WOULD BE VERY SMART.
MAYBE HE COULD SIT AND READ OR DISCUSS
TOPICS OF GREAT IMPORTANCE WITH LEADERS
FROM DIFFERENT LANDS.

IGUANAS ARE EDUCATIONAL!
WHEN MY CLASS HAS SHOW AND TELL DAYS
I COULD BRING MY IGUANA TO CLASS.
EUROPE
TEACHER

ANGELA IS A GIRL IN MY CLASS. SHE HAS TWO
IGUANAS. HER IGUANAS ARE BABIES RIGHT NOW.
SHE SAYS THEY WILL GROW TO BE VERY LARGE.
SHE LIKES TO LET THEM SIT ON HER HEAD.

MY IGUANA WOULD BE SO SPECIAL THAT EVERYONE FROM EVERYWHERE WILL WANT TO COME AND SEE IT.

MAYBE MY IGUANA COULD BE THE FIRST IGUANA IN SPACE, OR EVEN BE THE FIRST TO LAND ON MARS.
MARS NEEDS WOMEN

WHEN HE GOT BACK HOME
HE WOULD GET A PARADE FOR
BEING A HERO.

EVERYONE WOULD BE AMAZED AT HOW NICE AND GREEN HE IS. MAYBE HE COULD GET A MOVIE DEAL! MAYBE I COULD BE HIS AGENT !

**MY IGUANA WOULD GIVE
SPEECHES BEFORE COLLEGES
AND GATHERINGS OF PEOPLE
AND OTHER SMART IGUANAS
LIKE HIMSELF.**

**BUT YOU KNOW WHAT?
I DON'T THINK MY IGUANA WILL WANT
TO DO ANY OF THOSE THINGS.**

I THINK MY IGUANA WILL JUST WANT TO BE MY FRIEND.

THE CARE AND FEEDING OF IGUANAS

Iguanas grow very large and require much attention!
Talk with your parents and make sure you are ready and able to care for one.
Read everything you can before making a decision.

You must feed your Iguana every day. Iguanas are vegetarians.
Feed them chopped up fruits, and leafy green vegetables.
Vegetables like squash, zucchini, broccoli, and others are good too.
Fresh food at room temperature is best.

Give your Iguana fresh clean water in a shallow bowl.

Make sure your Iguana has plenty of living space.
Buy or build a good space for your Iguana to live in.
A 40 gallon aquarium is good to start with.

Keep the living space clean. Your Iguana does not like a dirty home.

Iguanas like nice warm areas; look into a special light from your pet supply store.

Take your Iguana to your Veterinarian for health checkups.

After you have cleaned your Iguana space and handled your Iguana, always remember to wash your hands with warm water and soap!

Take care when handling your Iguana.
Treat them with lots of love.
They love to be gently stroked.

Look on the internet for Iguana sites and learn more!

T.E. Watson is a childrens' book
author, computer instructor
and the V.P. of a Celtic software
company in Northern California
where he lives with his wife,Kim,
4 cats, and one Golden Retriever
named Samantha.

John Raptis lives in Sterling Heights,
Michigan, with his wife, Margaret, and
his dog, Bear, where he combines his
passions for reading and cartooning
with occasional forays into fine arts.
This is his first published work.

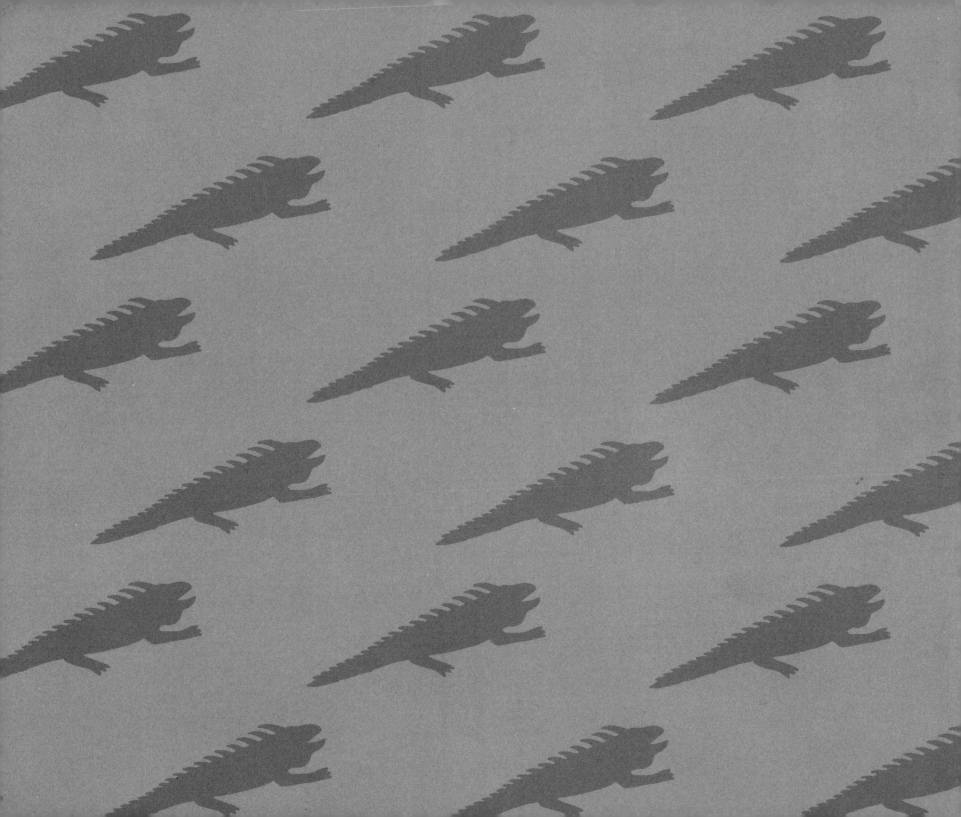